Judy Moody
SAVES THE WORLD!

Judy Moody
SAVES THE WORLD!

In a
World-Saving
MOod

Megan McDonald

illustrated by
Peter Reynolds

SCHOLASTIC INC.

New York Toronto London Auckland Sydney
Mexico City New Delhi Hong Kong Buenos Aires

ISBN 0-439-43174-3

12 11 10 9 8 7 6   3 4 5 6 7/0

Printed in the U.S.A.   40

First Scholastic printing, October 2002

This book was typeset in Stone Informal.
The illustrations were done in watercolor, tea, and pen and ink.

for Richard
—M. M.

for all the librarians
who believe a good story
can save the world!
—P. R.

Table of Contents

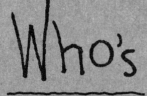

Who's

Judy

The heroine and garbologist,
famous for her many moods.

Dad

Judy's father.
Has a taste for rain
forest coffee beans.

Mom

Judy's mother.
Needs a lesson in recycling.

Mouse

Judy's cat.
Fond of bananas.

Stink

Judy's younger brother.
Batty about bats and Toady.

Who

Rocky

Judy's best friend since FOREVER. Hot on the trail of the Shenandoah salamander.

Toady

Endangered T. P. Club mascot.

Mr. Todd

Judy's teacher. Leader of the 3T ecosystem.

Frank

Judy's stamp-collecting friend. Knows a thing or two about monkeyface mussels.

Jessica

Judy's classmate. Pig fanatic and pencil freak.

Crazy Strips Contest

Judy Moody did not set out to save the world. She set out to win a contest. A Band-Aid contest.

Judy snapped open her doctor kit. Where was that box of Crazy Strips? She lifted out the tiny hammer for testing reflexes.

"Hey, can I try that?" asked Stink, coming into Judy's room.

"Stink, didn't you ever hear of going knock, knock?"

"Sure," said Stink. "Who's there?"

"Not the joke," said Judy. "The thing a little brother is supposed to do before entering a big sister's room."

"You mean I have to tell a joke just to come in your room?" asked Stink.

"Never mind," said Judy.

"Never mind who?" asked Stink.

"Stink! Just sit on the bed and cross your legs," said Judy. "I'm going to test your reflexes."

"Please don't do doctor stuff to me!" Stink said.

"C'mon, Stink." Judy tapped Stink's knee with the hammer. Stink's foot shot out and kicked her in the leg.

"Hey, Stink," said Judy. "You kicked me!

Who do you think you are, a cassowary?"

"A what-o-wary?"

"Cass-o-wary. I learned it in Science. It's a rain forest bird that can't fly, so it kicks its enemies."

"I'm not a casso-whatever," said Stink. "I just have really good reflexes."

Judy flashed her best anaconda eyes at Stink. "Forget it," she said, putting the hammer away.

Stink reached into Judy's doctor kit and pulled out some Crazy Strips.

"Stink! I told you not to steal my Crazy Strips. Now this box is empty, as in ALL GONE. I told you I'd put your arm in a sling if you didn't stop stealing my stuff."

Stink did not want his arm in a sling

again. Especially when it wasn't broken. "Give it," said Judy, taking the box from Stink. "I want to read about the contest."

"Contest?" asked Stink. "What do we have to do?"

Judy read the box.

Crazy Strips 5th Annual
Design Your Own Bandage Contest.

Create your own Crazy Strip.
Draw with pencils, crayons,
or markers.
Think of a theme.
Go wild with a style.
Be outrageous. Be you.

"You mean we draw something to go on a Crazy Strip?" asked Stink. "What do we win?"

Judy read on.

Thirteen top designs will be chosen to be
printed on Crazy Strips. Just think — kids all
across the country could be wearing YOUR
creative, colorful Crazy Strip.

"Is that all?" asked Stink.

"Rare!" Judy said. "I, Judy Moody, could
have my own Crazy Strip."

"They have to let you win something,"
Stink said, grabbing the box from Judy.

"Just think. Knees, ankles, and elbows
everywhere will be wearing a Judy Moody
original. Even Elizabeth Blackwell, First
Woman Doctor, didn't have her own Crazy
Strip."

"Oh, brother," said Stink. "Before you get too famous, can I use some of your skinny markers?"

"What for?" Judy asked.

"I want to draw a Crazy Strip, too. It says here the Grand Prize is a pair of Rollerblades."

"Rollerblades! Let me see that."

Top Winner: Crazy Strip of the Year
Rollerblades plus your design printed on a
Crazy Strip for one year

Runners-up: Crazy Strip of the Month
Crazy Strips sunglasses plus your design
printed on a Crazy Strip for one month

All participants receive Honorable Mention
certificates.

"Dream on, Stink. Only one kid in the whole entire United States of America gets Rollerblades."

"So?"

"So look at some of the kids who won last year. They're ten years old. Eleven. One is even thirteen. That's a teenager. You're only seven."

"And a quarter," said Stink.

"You'd have to be Picasso for them to pick your design," she said.

"Who?"

"You know. The guy who painted all those blue people."

"Then let me borrow your blue marker," said Stink.

Judy dumped all the markers, crayons,

colored pencils, and pastels she had on the floor. Stink grabbed the first blue marker he saw and started to draw.

"What are you drawing?"

"Bats," said Stink. "Blue bats."

"*You're* bats," said Judy. "People don't like bats."

"But bats eat millions of insects," said Stink. "People should like bats."

"I know *that*," said Judy. "I'm just saying, bats are not going to beat a teenager." Stink kept right on coloring bats.

"Your bats sure have big ears," said Judy.

"They're Virginia big-eared bats."

"Oh," said Judy.

Stink was a good artist, but Judy didn't

want him thinking he was a genius or any-thing. She had to dream up a good-as-Picasso idea. Better than ucky old bats. Better than a teenager. She wanted her Judy Moody Crazy Strip to be seen all across the U.S.A. The world. The universe.

"Stink, stop squeaking," said Judy.

"It's the magic markers."

"I can't think with all that squeaking," Judy said.

Judy studied some of the other winners on the box from last year. There were lady-bugs, flowers, soccer balls, rainbows, and peace signs. Happy, happy, happy. Judy tried to think of something happy to draw on her Crazy Strip.

She drew smiley faces. Yellow, red, blue, green, and purple smiley faces. Underneath she wrote CRAZY STRIPS CURE BAD MOODS.

"Everybody draws smiley faces," said Stink.

"Who?" asked Judy.

"Heather Strong, in my class. And teenagers."

Stink was right. Smiley faces were not good enough to decorate the ankles of millions. Smiley faces were not good enough to win Rollerblades. Smiley faces were not Picasso.

Judy turned her Crazy Strip upside down. The smiley faces turned into bad-mood faces.

"Nobody wants a cranky Crazy Strip," Stink said.

"ROAR!" said Judy.

"They like it if you have a message," said Stink, "but I can't think of a message about bats."

"How about BATTY FOR BAND-AIDS?"

"That's good!" said Stink. "Thanks!"

Stink was already done with his Crazy Strip and Judy still did not have a single idea. Not one inspiration.

"Okay, let's go mail this," said Stink.

Fresh air! That was it! Maybe Judy's brain just needed some good old-fashioned oxygen.

On the way to the mailbox, Stink asked, "Do you think I'll win?"

"What am I? A crystal ball?" asked Judy.

"How long do you think it takes?" asked Stink, dropping the envelope into the big blue box.

"Longer than one second," said Judy.

On the way home, Judy gulped in fresh air.

"You look like a goldfish in a toilet," Stink said.

It was no use. Fresh air was not helping. Fresh air just made her look like a toilet fish.

Stink's Crazy Strip was already in the mail. What if Stink won the contest? What if she could never ever even come up with an idea?

She, Judy Moody, was in a mood.

Batty for Banana Peels

All day Saturday and all day Sunday, Judy could not think up one single creative, award-winning Crazy Strips idea. On Monday morning, as soon as she got to the bus stop, Judy told her best friend, Rocky, about the contest. "Help me think of an idea!"

"I know," said Rocky. "How about a disappearing one? You put it on your arm, only it's clear, so it's invisible."

"Rare!" said Judy. "A disappearing Crazy Strip! That's good!"

"How are you going to win the contest if they can't even see it?" Stink asked.

"Good point," said Judy, thinking it over. "I want the world to be able to *see* my Grand Prize–winning Judy Moody Crazy Strip."

⊚   ⊚   ⊚

At school, Judy was dying to ask Frank Pearl if he had any ideas, but the bell had already rung and she could not risk getting another white card for talking. She already had to stay after school once and clean the fish tank with Mr. Todd for getting three white cards. A person could only clean so many stinky fish tanks.

So she wrote a note about the contest to pass to Frank instead. At the bottom she wrote: *P. S. DON'T let Jessica Finch see this.*

"Science, everybody," said Mr. Todd. "Let's continue our discussion of the environment. Rain forests everywhere are being cut down. When you take medicine or bounce a ball or pop a balloon, you're using something that came from the rain forest. And right here at home, malls are replacing trees, animals are disappearing, and we're running out of places to put all of our trash.

"Today, let's come up with ways we can help save the earth. Sometimes it's good to start small. Think of ways we can help at home. In our own families. And at school. Any ideas?"

"Don't leave lights on," said Hailey.

"Recycle your homework," said Frank.

"And cans and bottles and stuff," said Leo.

"Turn garbage into dirt," said Rocky.

"Yes," said Mr. Todd. "That's called composting."

Judy raised her hand, knocking her note to the floor. "Plant trees!"

"Don't be litterbugs," said Jessica Finch.

"I wasn't littering," said Judy, picking up the note. She crossed out the Finch in Jessica's name and changed it to Jessica Fink. Sheesh. Sometimes Jessica Fink Finch gave her the jitterbugs.

"Great!" said Mr. Todd. "These are all good ideas. Look around you — at home, in school, on the playground — not just in Science class. How can we help the planet? How can we make the world around us a better place? We can each do our part. All it takes is one person to make a difference."

One person! If all it took was one person, then she, Judy Moody, could save the world!

She knew just where to start. With a banana peel.

❧   ❧   ❧

On the way home from school that afternoon, Judy asked Rocky, "Hey, can you come over and eat some bananas?"

"Sure," said Rocky. "What for?"

"Compost," said Judy.

"I'll eat two!" said Rocky.

In Judy's kitchen, Judy and Rocky each ate one and a half bananas. They fed the fourth and last one to Mouse, Judy's cat. Then Judy tossed all four banana peels into a bucket.

"Why don't we make a sign for the bucket that says TURN GARBAGE INTO DIRT," said Rocky.

"Rare!" said Judy. "Tomorrow we can tell Mr. Todd how we started to heal the world."

"Double cool," said Rocky.

"Wait just a minute," said Judy. "Why didn't I think of it before? HEAL THE WORLD! That's it!"

"What's it?"

"My Band-Aid. For the Crazy Strips contest! You'll see." Judy ran upstairs and came back with markers and some paper. At the kitchen table, Rocky made a sign for the compost bucket while Judy drew a picture of Earth with a Band-Aid on it. She wrote HEAL THE WORLD under the globe in her best not-in-cursive letters. Then she drew banana peels all around the world.

Stink came into the kitchen. "What are you drawing?" he asked Judy.

"Banana peels," said Judy.

"For the Crazy Strip Contest," Rocky said.

"And you thought bats were weird?" said Stink. "Bats aren't half as crazy as banana peels."

He looked at the empty bowl on the table. "Hey! Who ate the last banana?"

"Mouse!" said Judy. Judy and Rocky fell on the floor laughing.

"No way," said Stink.

"Just look at her whiskers," said Judy.

Stink got down on the floor, face to face

with the cat. "Gross! Mouse has banana smoosh on her whiskers."

"Told you," said Judy.

"I'm telling Mom you ate all the bananas," said Stink. "And you fed one to Mouse."

"Tell her it's all in the name of science," said Judy. "You'll see. From now on there are going to be a few changes around here."

"We're making compost," said Rocky. "See?" He held up his sign.

"It takes like a hundred years to turn garbage into dirt," said Stink.

"Stink, *you're* going to be dirt. Unless you make like a tree and leaf us alone."

A Mr. Rubbish Mood

It was still dark out when Judy woke up early the next morning. She found her flashlight and notebook. Then she tiptoed downstairs to the kitchen and started to save the world.

She hoped she could save the world before breakfast. Judy wondered if other people making the world a better place had to do it quietly, and in the dark, so their parents would not wake up.

She, Judy Moody, was in a Mr. Rubbish mood. Mr. Rubbish was the Good Garbage Gremlin in Stink's comic book, who built his house out of French-fry cartons and pop bottles. He recycled everything, even lollipop sticks. And he never used anything from the rain forest.

Hmm . . . things that came from the rain forest. That would be a good place to start. Rubber came from the rain forest. And chocolate and spices and things like perfume. Even chewing gum.

Judy collected stuff from around the house and piled it on the kitchen table. Chocolate bars, brownie mix, vanilla ice cream. Her dad's coffee beans. The rubber toilet plunger. Gum from Stink's gumball machine. Her mom's lipstick from the bottom of her purse. She was so busy saving the rain forest that she didn't hear her family come into the kitchen.

"What in the world . . . ?" Mom said.

"Judy, why are you in the dark?" Dad asked, turning on the lights.

"Hey, my gumball machine!" Stink said.

Judy held out her arms to block the way. "We're not going to use this stuff anymore. It's all from the rain forest," she told them.

"Says who?" asked Stink.

"Says Mr. Rubbish. And Mr. Todd. They cut down way too many trees to grow coffee and give us makeup and chewing gum.

Mr. Todd says the earth is our home. We have to take action to save it. We don't need all this stuff."

"I need gum!" yelled Stink. "Give me back my gum!"

"Stink! Don't yell. Haven't you ever heard of noise pollution?"

"Is my coffee in there?" Dad asked, rubbing his hair.

"Judy? Is that ice cream? It's dripping all over the table!" Mom carried the leaky carton over to the sink.

"ZZZZ-ZZZZZ!" Judy made the sound of a chain saw cutting down trees.

"She's batty," Stink said.

Dad put the brownie mix back in the cupboard. Mom took the toilet plunger off the kitchen table and headed for the bath-room.

Time for Plan B. Project R. E. C. Y. C. L. E. She, Judy Moody, would show her family just how much they hurt the planet. Every time someone threw something away, she would write it down. She got her notebook and looked in the trash can. She wrote down:

1 orange juice can
1 inside of peanut butter jar lid
1 plastic bread bag
4 broken eggshells
smelly yucky wet coffee grounds
3 paper muffin holders
2 smooshed Scarlett O'cherry Juice Boxes (and straws!)
½ bowl of oatmeal

"Stink! You shouldn't throw gooey old oatmeal in the trash!" Judy said.

"Dad! Tell her to quit spying on me."

"I'm a Garbage Detective!" said Judy. "*Garbologist* to you. Mr. Todd says if you want to learn what to recycle, you have to get to know your garbage."

"Here," said Stink, sticking something wet and mushy under Judy's nose. "Get to know my apple core."

"Hardee har har," said Judy. "Hasn't anybody in this family ever heard of the Three R's?"

"The Three R's?" asked Dad.

"Re-use. Re-cycle."

"What's the third one?" asked Stink.

"Re-fuse to talk to little brothers until they quit throwing stuff away."

"Mom! I'm not going to stop throwing stuff away just because Judy's having a trash attack."

"Look at all this stuff we throw away!" Judy said. "Did you know that one person throws away more than eight pounds of garbage a day?"

"We recycle all our glass and cans," said Mom.

"And newspapers," Dad said.

"But what about this?" said Judy, picking a plastic bag out of the trash. This bread bag could be a purse! Or carry a library book."

"What's so great about eggshells?" asked Stink. "And smelly old ground-up coffee?"

"You can use them to feed plants. Or make compost." Just then, something in the trash caught her eye. A pile of Popsicle sticks? Judy pulled it out. "Hey! My Laura Ingalls Wilder log cabin I made in second grade!"

"It looks like a glue museum to me," said Stink.

"I'm sorry, Judy," Mom said. "I should have asked first, but we can't save everything, honey."

"Recycle it!" said Stink. "You could use it for kindling, to start a fire! Or break it down into toothpicks."

"Not funny, Stink."

"Judy, you're not even ready for school yet. Let's talk about this later," said Dad. "It's time to get dressed."

It was no use. Nobody listened to her. Judy trudged upstairs, feeling like a sloth without a tree.

"I won't wear lipstick today if it'll make you feel better," Mom called up the stairs.

"And I'll only drink half a cup of coffee," Dad said, but Judy could hardly hear him over the grinding of the rain forest coffee beans.

Her family sure knew how to ruin a perfectly good Mr. Rubbish mood. She put on her jeans and her Spotted Owl T-shirt. And to save water, she did not brush her teeth.

She clomped downstairs in a mad-at-your-whole-family mood.

"Here's your lunch," said Mom.

"Mom! It's in a paper bag!"

"What's wrong with that?" Stink asked.

"Don't you get it?" said Judy. "They cut down trees to make paper bags. Trees give shade. They help control global warming. We would die without trees. They make oxygen and help take dust and stuff out of the air."

"Dust!" said Mom. "Let's talk about cleaning your room if we're going to talk dust."

"Mo-om!" How was she supposed to do important things like save trees if she couldn't even save her *family* tree? That did it. Judy went straight to the garage and dug out her Sleeping Beauty lunch box from kindergarten.

"Are you really going to take that baby lunch box on the bus? Where the whole world can see?" asked Stink.

"I'm riding my bike today," said Judy. "To save energy."

"See you at school, then." Stink waved his *paper-bag* lunch at her. If only she could recycle her little brother.

"Go ahead. Be a tree hater," called Judy. "It's your funeral."

Making the world a better place sure was complicated.

Pigtoes, Pumas, and Pimplebacks

At school, Judy wiggled all during Math in the morning. She squirmed through Spelling. At last it was Science.

"Over half the world's plants and animals are found in rain forests," Mr. Todd said. "Which is why it's so important to protect the rain forest. The health of our whole planet depends on it. But did you know that there are endangered species right here in Virginia?"

Endangered species! Right here in Virginia! Judy leaned forward in her seat.

"If we want to take care of our planet, it helps to begin in our own backyard. That's why I'm asking each of you to adopt an endangered animal from Virginia this week. Tell us about the species, why it's disappearing, and what can be done to help."

Adopt an animal! She could help an endangered species. She, Judy Moody, could help save the entire state of Virginia!

Mr. Todd was shaking a coffee can. "Each slip of paper has the name of one endangered animal on it. When I call on you, come up and take one slip of paper from the can. Who wants to be first?"

All hands went up in the air.

"Rocky."

"Shenandoah salamander!" said Rocky, reading his slip of paper.

"Frank Pearl."

"Monkeyface mussel!"

Rare! Judy waved her hand in the air like a flag. Mr. Todd still did not call on her.

Brad got the bald eagle. Hailey got the puma. Randi got the leatherback sea turtle.

"Jessica Finch."

"Shiny pigtoe," said Jessica. "Yippee!"

Judy could not think of anybody else who would want to adopt a pig's toe. Only Jessica Finch. Jessica Finch liked everything about pigs. Even shiny pigs' toes.

While Mr. Todd called out more names, Judy turned around and said to Jessica,

"A shiny pigtoe is a pig with nail polish!" She cracked herself up.

"Judy Moody."

Judy turned around, her hand the only one still left in the air. "One left," said Mr. Todd. "C'mon up."

Finally! Judy unfolded the small slip of paper. "Northeast beach tiger beetle," she read.

Northeast beach tiger beetle! A northeast beach tiger beetle was not even an animal. It was a bug. An icketty cricketty old creepy crawly.

"If we don't like ours, can we trade?" Judy asked.

"I'd like everybody to stick with their choices," said Mr. Todd.

"What if we never even heard of it? What if we don't even know what it looks like?" said Judy.

"That's the fun of it," said Mr. Todd. "Find out. Go to the library and look at books and magazines. Or search the Web at the computer lab. And this Thursday, we'll be taking a class field trip to the museum, which should have information on all of your adopted animals."

"Big museum or little museum?" asked Frank.

"Little," said Mr. Todd. The class groaned.

The big museum meant the Smithsonian in Washington, D.C. Or the one with all the planes. The little museum meant the science museum down the street. It had toy trains, plastic dinosaurs, and one-hundred-year-old pictures of Virginia stuff.

"The best exhibit there is cobwebs," Rocky said.

෧   ෧   ෧

When Thursday came, Judy wore her tiger-striped pajama pants to school in honor of the tiger beetle. At the museum, Mr. Todd introduced the class to the museum lady. "This is Ms. Stickley, and she's going to tell us about endangered species in Virginia."

Ms. Stickley looked like a stick bug. Even her socks were brown.

"Call me Stephanie," said Ms. Stick Bug.

"Class," said Mr. Todd. "I expect you to give Stephanie your best third-grade listening ears." Frank pretended to take off his ears and hand them to her. Judy cracked up.

Ms. Stephanie Stick Bug took them on a tour of *Where the Wild Things Aren't*. She showed them a real live Shenandoah salamander, a Virginia fringed mountain snail that looked extremely sluggy, and a stuffed flying squirrel glued to a board.

"A flying squirrel! Is his name Rocky, like in *Rocky and Bullwinkle?*" asked Frank.

"Yes," said Ms. Stick Bug. "As a matter of fact it is."

"His name is Rocky, too!" said Frank, pointing at Rocky. "Hey, Rocky, you're a squirrel!"

"And you're Bullwinkle!" said Rocky. "You're a moose! Ha!"

Judy was dying to ask Ms. Stick Bug a

question. She raised her hand, holding it as straight as a shortnose sturgeon. At last, Stephanie called on her.

"Do you have any northeast beach tiger beetles?" asked Judy.

"No, I'm sorry we don't," said Stephanie. "Those *are* endangered in Virginia and that would be a good specimen for our collection."

What kind of endangered species museum did not have any northeast beach tiger beetles?

"Do you have any cave isopods?" asked Jessica Smartypants Finch.

"What's an ice-o-pod?" asked Rocky.

"An isopod is a crustacean like a sow bug," answered Stephanie. "Think of it like a pill bug, or a wood louse. You'll find those in Arachnid Hall."

"Ick! A louse is lice!" said Rocky.

Judy still couldn't see why they didn't have any northeast beach tiger beetles. After all, they had a bunch of creepy crustaceans, licey isopods, and pillbuggy pests.

Judy raised her hand again. She wanted to sound as smart as Jessica Finch.

"Excuse me," she said. "Do you have any two-toed sloths here? Tropical treehoppers? Nocturnal aye-ayes?"

"We don't have a rain forest exhibit," said Ms. Stick Bug. "But it's a great idea. Maybe someday."

The whole class got to touch an orangefoot pimpleback pearlymussel shell and hear a story about a Dismal Swamp shrew.

"Everything in this whole place is endangered," said Frank.

"My grade in Science is endangered, too," said Judy.

Beetle Emergency

The very next morning, Judy started her own search for a real live northeast beach tiger beetle. Before school, she grabbed a peanut butter jar from the recycling bin and ran out into the backyard. She tapped on tree bark. She crawled through itchy grass. She peered down into the dirt.

"Here, beetle, beetle," called Judy. "Don't be endangered."

She did not find one single beetle. All she found was an acorn hat, a slug, and a not-recycled candy wrapper.

"Judy!" called her Dad. "What are you doing out there in your pajamas?"

"Looking for a northeast beach tiger beetle," said Judy. "They're endangered. Mr. Todd says saving endangered species begins in your own backyard," said Judy.

"Not before breakfast in your pajamas," said Dad. "All the beetles are still sleeping."

At school that day, Judy searched for a picture of her beetle. And a few facts. She looked in the dictionary. She looked in the encyclopedia. She looked in bug books. She even looked on the computer. No luck.

Most of the beetles in the computer were the John Lennon and Paul McCartney kind of Beatles.

❧ ❧ ❧

The next day was Saturday. Frank Pearl called Judy. "Can I come over?"

"Not unless you bring a northeast beach tiger beetle with you."

"Okay," said Frank.

"You found one?" Judy asked. "For real?"

"Not a live one. But I found a picture of one. Do you have any stamps at your house?" asked Frank.

"What's stamps got to do with any-thing?"

"Just go see if you have any stamps. Stamps with bugs."

Judy put down the phone and ran to find some stamps in her parents' desk.

"Just boring old flags," she told Frank.

"Well, I have gazillions of stamps and—"

"How come you have so many stamps?"

"I collect them. I was pasting some in my album when I saw your beetle on one of the stamps."

"Bring it over right away," said Judy. "Tell your mom it's an emergency."

Half an hour later, Frank rang the doorbell. "Finally!" said Judy, pulling him into the living room.

Frank put his stamp album on the coffee table and opened it up. He turned to the Insects and Spiders page. "Look at all the

beetles," said Frank. "That's a lady beetle—those are good luck. And there's a dung beetle, a Hercules beetle, and a spotted water beetle. Even an elderberry longhorn beetle."

"Which one is it?" Judy shrieked. Frank pointed to a beetle with a shiny green head and eyes like an alien. Printed below the beetle it said *Cicindela dorsalis dorsalis*.

"That's not a northeast beach tiger beetle," said Judy. "It's some kind of a Cinderella beetle."

"It's Latin," said Frank.

"Latin? Don't they have any beetles that speak English?"

"Read what it says underneath."

Northeast beach tiger beetle. Found along sandy beaches in the Chesapeake Bay areas of Virginia. Endangered by changes in habitat, human population, shoreline development, and erosion.

"My beetle's a beach bum! Thanks a million gazillion, Frank. Now I can work on my report. First I'll draw a picture for the cover."

"Want some help?" asked Frank.

"Sure," said Judy. "You can put the caps back on the markers."

Judy drew many-legged northeast beach tiger beetles all over the cover of her report. "Make sure they have biting mouth parts," said Frank. "And wings."

"Oh, yeah," said Judy.

"Can I help color them in?" asked Frank.

"Okay. Thanks," Judy said. "Did you already draw your cover for the monkey-face mussel?"

"Yeah," said Frank. "It's a seashell with bumps on it that look like a monkey's face. No lie. You can see eyes and ears and everything."

"I got to see that," said Judy. She printed the title of her report in all capitals. SAVE THE NORTHEAST BEACH TIGER BEETLE.

"Rare!" said Judy.

"Double cool," said Frank.

Just as she finished her cover, Stink came into the room and looked at Judy's drawing. "Why did you draw fat, flying footballs all over your report?"

Pond Scum

Judy worked on her report all weekend. In Science on Monday, the class presented its endangered species. Frank told the class how a monkeyface mussel got its name. Jessica Finch showed a shiny pigtoe shell that looked like a striped Hershey's Kiss. Judy bragged about the importance of the northeast beach tiger beetle.

"Tiger beetles recycle dead trees and eat tons of harmful insects, so don't step on

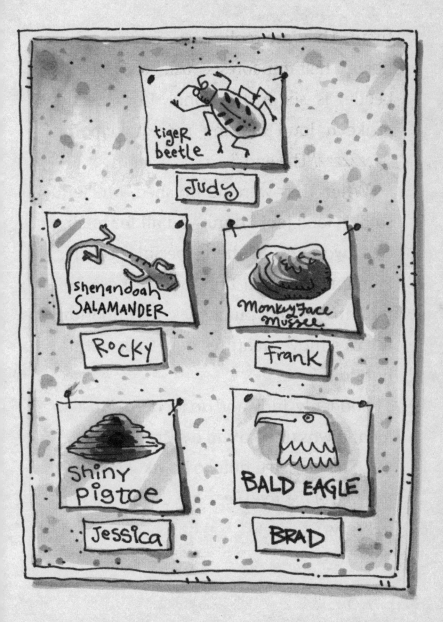

them. They are really fast and tricky, like tigers. Their rain forest cousin, the Hercules beetle, is six inches long! Tiger beetles make a loud buzzing sound, like this. *Bzzzzzzzz!* The end."

When they were all finished, Mr. Todd said, "Good job! Thank you all for raising our awareness of these special creatures. Remember, if you find one of these animals in the wild, put it back. It's important not to remove creatures from their natural habitats."

Suddenly, Judy had an idea. An Einstein idea! It was time to call a secret club meeting. She passed a note to Frank: *Emergency meeting of the Toad Pee Club. Today! Pass this to Rocky.*

Emergency meeting of the Toad Pee Club today! Pass this to Rocky -J.M.

Jessica leaned forward, trying to see Judy's note. "I'll bet you can't spell the word *endangered*," hissed Jessica.

"Yes I can," said Judy. "G-O-N-E, gone."

Judy had ants in her pants all through Spelling.

Bzzzzzzz! At last the bell rang, like a sweet chorus of buzzing tiger beetles, and she, Judy Moody, was G-O-N-E, gone.

᭡   ᭡   ᭡

After school, Frank, Rocky, and Judy crawled inside the blue tent in Judy's backyard. While they waited for Stink, Judy whispered the plan to Frank and Rocky.

"I'll get rid of Stink," said Rocky.

"And I'll keep an eye on Toady," said Frank. Finally, Stink crawled inside the tent, carrying Toady, their mascot, in a yogurt container.

"Where are we gonna put Toady?" asked Stink.

"Over here in the corner by me," said Frank. "I'll guard him."

"And don't pick him up with your bare hands, Stink, or he'll get you. *If* you know what I mean," Judy warned him.

"Hey, did you know if you change two letters around in *T-o-a-d-y* you get *t-o-d-a-y*?" asked Stink.

"That's nice, Stink," said Judy. "Did you know if you add three letters to Stink you get Stinkbug?"

Stink ignored her. "It's squishy in here," he complained.

"Try making yourself a little smaller, Stink. People take up way too much room on the planet. That's why we have so many problems."

"Oh brother," said Stink. "Why are we here anyway?"

"No reason," said Rocky. He kicked Frank's shoe and Frank nudged Judy and all three cracked up.

"Let's brainstorm," said Frank. "You know, think up stuff we can do in our club.

Even though it's really hot and crowded in here."

"I'm too squished. It's too hot in here to brainstorm," said Stink.

"It's global warming," said Judy. "Right here in Virginia."

Stink panted like a dog. "Stink. Don't breathe so much. You'll ruin the ozone," said Judy. "There's already a hole over Antarctica!"

"You're in the ozone," said Stink. He crawled out of the tent.

"Perfect!" said Judy. Judy, Rocky, and Frank double high-fived each other.

"And he forgot to take Toady!" said Rocky.

"T-o-d-a-y is your lucky day, T-o-a-d-y.

Today is the day we save the world, starting with you," Judy said.

Frank picked up Toady. Toady blinked. "He doesn't look endangered!"

"No, but your hand is endangered," said Judy. "Better put him back."

"I kind of hate to see him go," said Frank.

"But Mr. Todd said! Remember? If you catch a creature in the wild you have to put it back. Toadnapping is the same thing as hurting the planet," Judy explained.

"Just think how happy he'll be," said Rocky.

They carried Toady down to the stream behind Judy's house. "I'll miss you, Toady," Judy said. "But the time has come for you to join your toady friends and do your

toady things. Go make this planet a better place." On the count of three, Judy, Rocky, and Frank gently tipped the yogurt container on its side and let Toady go.

"Goodbye, Toadster!" said Rocky.

"Watch out for acid rain!" said Frank. Toady blinked once, then *bloomp!* He plopped into the water. In one, two, three bubbles, Toady was gone.

"Nice sendoff," said Frank.

"It's for a good cause," said Rocky.

"Toadly awesome!" said Judy.

Rocky and Frank went home. She, Judy Moody, was on her way to making the world a better place. The Toad Pee Club had taken one small step for toadkind and one giant leapfrog for humankind.

⊚ ⊚ ⊚

It took Stink one hour and twenty-eight minutes to notice that Toady was missing. Endangered, as in G-O-N-E, gone.

"Toady's gone?" asked Stink. "Oh, no! What if he got swallowed by a snake? Or gobbled by a giant hawk? It's all my fault for leaving him in the tent. Why didn't you *do* something?"

"I did," said Judy, and she broke the good news about letting Toady go to make the planet a better place.

If Stink were a poison dart frog, he would have spit poison at Judy. If Stink were a volcano, he would have spewed lava.

"It's not fair!" Stink moaned. "Toady was my pet!"

"Toady belonged to all the members of the Toad Pee Club."

"But I took care of him mostly," said Stink. "How can letting him go make the world a better place? It makes it a worse place if you ask me."

"Stink, you'd be pond scum if you kept Toady locked up in that aquarium," said

Judy. "That aquarium is like being in jail."

"*You're* gonna be in jail as soon as I tell Mom and Dad."

"Look at it this way. Toady gets to be free and now there will be even more toads. Don't you get it?"

"I get that you stole my toad."

Sometimes Stink could be as stubborn as a hard-headed hornbill.

"Now we don't even have a mascot for our club," said Stink.

Judy grabbed Mouse. "Mouse could be our new mascot!"

"The Mouse Pee Club? I don't think so," said Stink. "See? If it wasn't for Toady, there wouldn't even be a Toad Pee Club."

"There will be other toads to pee on us, Stink. I promise."

"I'm still telling," said Stink.

Luna Two

The next day, Judy came home from school and climbed a tree.

She, Judy Moody, was in Trouble with a capital T. Why was her whole family mad at her for letting a toad go free? She was just doing her part to save the world.

Stink saw her up in the tree. "Hey. No fair! Mom and Dad said you had to go straight to your room!"

"This *is* my room," Judy said. "I'm going to live up here now. Like Julia Butterfly Hill."

"Who?"

"The girl who lived in a tree for two years. Mr. Todd told us. They were going to cut down some ancient redwoods in California. So Julia Butterfly Hill climbed one of the trees and stayed there. They couldn't cut down a tree with a person in it. She even named the tree Luna."

"You can't just live in a tree, Judy," said Stink.

"Judy Monarch Moody to you."

"Oh, brother," said Stink.

"If I live in this tree, newspapers will come. And TV people. Everybody will learn how important trees are. I'll call my tree Luna Two."

"How about luna-tic," said Stink.

"Hardee-har-har," said Judy. "Stink, you will have to be the gofer."

"Gopher? A gopher sounds like a rat."

"An *important* rat," said Judy. "Go get me my walkie-talkies. It will be like Julia Butterfly Hill's solar-powered cell phone. That's how I'll talk to people."

Stink came back with the walkie-talkies. Judy climbed down to a lower branch and Stink stood on a milk crate to pass them up to her.

"Now get me a flashlight. It's going to get dark up here."

Stink went and got the flashlight.

"Now can you get me a glass of water?" asked Judy.

"Water? What's the water for?" asked Stink.

"I'm thirsty!"

"Forget it," said Stink.

"I'll pay you fifty cents."

"How long are you going to be up there?" Stink asked, thinking of all the money he could make.

"Julia Butterfly Hill was in her tree for seven hundred and thirty-eight days. Sooner or later, Stink, you're going to have to get me some water. And lentils. Julia Butterfly Hill ate lentils."

"Lentils! You never ate a lentil in your life!" Stink said. He got a bottle of water.

"You owe me fifty cents," said Stink. "We're all out of lentils. I forgot I used them to make my Empire State Building in Social Studies."

"I guess I'll learn to like lima beans," said Judy. "Ick."

"Rocky's on his way over," said Stink. "He called and I told him you live in a tree now. I told him you are going to be in big trouble when Mom and Dad find out you didn't go straight to your room."

"This *is* my room."

"Then can I have your room inside the house?"

❧　　❧　　❧

Rocky raced around the corner into the backyard. "What's up, Judy? Besides you, I mean?" He cracked himself up.

Judy didn't laugh. Judy didn't say a word.

"You have to call her Judy Monarch Moody," said Stink.

"Oh, I get it," said Rocky. "Like that girl who lived in the tree. What are you going to do if it rains?"

"I'll stay under the leaves," said Judy.

"What about when it gets dark?" asked Rocky.

"I have a flashlight," said Judy.

"See what I mean?" said Stink. "First she went crazy over some trash. Then it was a weird beetle. She's driving *me* up a tree!"

"Oh, no! Not you too?" Rocky and Stink fell on the ground laughing.

"How are we going to get her to come down?" Stink asked Rocky.

"Mr. Todd said the tree cutters tried playing loud music and shining bright lights at Julia Butterfly Hill all night to make her come down," said Rocky.

"Time for Operation Boom Box," said Stink.

They blasted loud music to annoy Judy into coming down. She just put her hands over her ears and hummed "O Beautiful for Spacious Skies."

"What else did they try on Julia?" asked Stink.

"Lawsuits," said Rocky.

"I'll sue you if you don't come down!" yelled Stink.

"For what?" asked Judy.

"For staying up in a tree and getting out of your punishment or something."

"Or something," said Judy.

"Let's try shaking the tree," said Rocky. They put their hands around the tree and shook, but the tree did not budge one leaf.

"Tree bark is worse than bug bites," Stink said, showing his scraped-up arm. "Hey, Judy, I need a doctor. For real. Go get your doctor kit."

"Nice try," said Judy Monarch Moody.

Just then, Mouse came outside and bolted up the tree.

"Thanks for the company," called Judy. "Now I won't get lonely up here."

"Great," said Stink. "Now Mouse won't come down either. And we'll have to call her Mouse Swallowtail Moody or something."

"I have to stay up here," said Judy. "For the sake of all trees. And owls and flying squirrels and all the things that need trees. Even people. And toads."

"Let's just leave her up there," said Stink. "Who cares if she falls? Who cares if she gets in big trouble?"

"Even Judy Monarch Moody can't stay up there forever. You have to go to school," called Rocky.

"Julia Butterfly Hill got a Ph.D. from a college while she was up in the tree," Judy called back.

"Maybe if we ignore her she'll come down," said Rocky.

"Operation Ignore Judy," said Stink.

Stink and Rocky went inside. Mouse leaped down from a branch and followed them. "Traitor!" Judy yelled after her cat.

Living in a tree was a little lonely. Judy wondered if Julia Butterfly Hill got lonely, too. Seven hundred and thirty-eight days was a long time. Judy had hardly lasted seven hundred and thirty-eight seconds.

◈   ◈   ◈

A few minutes later, Stink and Rocky ran

back outside. Stink waved an envelope in the air. "Hey you, up there," said Stink. "Judy Monarch Moody."

"What now?" asked Judy.

"You got a letter from the Crazy Strips Contest!" Rocky yelled up at her.

"Really?" said Judy, looking down from her perch. "Open it and read it to me."

"No way," said Stink. "You have to come down and find out for yourself."

"I'm not going to fall for that trick, Stink," said Judy.

"I'll read it," said Stink. He opened the envelope. He unfolded the letter. *"Dear Judy Moody,"* read Stink. "I guess they don't know your middle name is Monarch."

"Just read it!" said Judy.

"Congratulations! You are a winner of the Crazy Strips Design Your Own Bandage Contest."

Judy could not believe her ears! She dropped down from her branch in Luna

Two like a leopard to its prey. "Let me see that!" Out loud, she read,

Dear Judy Moody,
We miss your smile.
Please call us to schedule
an appointment with
the dentist at your earliest

SMILEY DENTAL

Stink and Rocky cracked up as bad as a Brazil nut.

"STINK!" Judy wailed. "You tricked me. This is not from the Crazy Strips Company. You got me out of my tree because the dentist missed my smile?"

"It worked," said Stink.

"Take a good look at this smile," said

Judy, baring her teeth, Siberian tiger–style.

"Does this mean I can't have your room?" asked Stink.

"ROAR!" said Judy.

Batty for Band-Aids

When Judy, Stink, and Rocky got off the bus after school the next day, Stink called, "Race you to the mailbox!" But Judy did not run after Stink. She stayed right where she was so she could watch Rocky do his new disappearing-bubble-gum trick. That's when they heard Stink yell from across the street, "The Crazy Strips Contest! Judy, you won!" He waved an envelope in the air.

"Stink, you lie like a rug!" Judy said. "I'm not falling for that trick again."

"It says CONTEST WINNER. Right here in fat red letters. See?"

"If this is a trick, *you're* up a tree," Judy said, crossing the street.

"Maybe it's not a trick this time," said Rocky, walking beside her. "What did she win?"

"Rollerblades!" said Stink.

"Rollerblades do not fit in an envelope, Stink."

"Maybe you're a runner-up, then," said Stink. "Maybe you won sunglasses."

"Sunglasses don't fit in an envelope either. Give it." Judy grabbed the envelope and tore it open.

Dear Ms. Moody,
Congratulations! Enclosed
please find an Honorable Mention
Certificate for entering our Crazy
Strips Contest. Great job!

OFFICIAL

M.J. Donovan
CRAZY STRIPS C.E.O.

"Certificate?" yelled Judy. "That's all I get for HEAL THE WORLD? One crummy certificate? A certificate is not even close to Rollerblades. A certificate will not decorate the ankles of millions."

"An Honorable Mention certificate is like winning second place," said Rocky.

Judy covered up her ears. "Don't even *mention* the word certificate again."

"At least you got *something*," Stink said.

"Yeah," Rocky said. "Stink didn't even get a certificate."

That cheered Judy up a little. "Well, at least I get to hang something in the Moody Hall of Fame on the fridge."

Just then, Stink dropped the mail. Catalogs and envelopes blew every which way. "Help!" yelled Stink. A letter flew out from inside a catalog and landed on the driveway.

"Wait!" called Stink, picking up the letter. "I got one too!"

"Let's see if you still think certificates are so great," said Judy.

Stink took his time opening the envelope.

"Stink, I'll be in fourth grade by the time you get that open. Hurry up. Read it!"

Stink read the letter.

Dear Mr. Moody,

Congratulations! You are a winner in the Crazy Strips Design Your Own Bandage Contest! Your design, Batty for Band-Aids, will be a featured Crazy Strip of the Month for October.

M. L. Donovan
CRAZY STRIPS C.E.O.

"Crazy Strip of the Month!" said Stink, jumping up and down and waving the letter in the air. "I got Crazy Strip of the Month!"

"Let me see that." Judy read the letter with her own eyes. How could this happen? Her very own stinky little brother won Crazy Strip of the Month!

"What's wrong with these people?" cried Judy, shaking the letter. Did they have bats in their belfries? Band-Aids for brains? "Don't they know bats have beady little eyes and squished-up noses like pigs? Don't they know bats look like vampires?"

"At least they don't look like flying footballs," said Stink.

"Don't they even care about healing the world?" Judy said.

"Big-eared bats are endangered," said Stink. "Putting them on a Crazy Strip is like healing the world."

"ROAR!" said Judy. Big-eared bats were going to decorate the ankles of millions. Meanwhile, the entire state of Virginia would be stepping on northeast beach tiger beetles and not even knowing it.

"Hey! What about your Rollerblades?" asked Rocky.

"It says here I won a pair of Crazy Strips sunglasses," said Stink.

"That must be your prize," said Rocky, pointing to a big box on the porch. Stink and Rocky ran over, with Judy right behind them.

"It's from the Crazy Strips company!" said Stink. "My sunglasses!"

"They must be sunglasses for a rhino," said Judy.

"Maybe they messed up and sent you Rollerblades by mistake," said Rocky.

"I hope they're black with a red racing stripe and a silver—"

"Stink! Just open the box!" said Judy.

Stink ripped into the box. It was not Rollerblades. It was not sunglasses for a rhino. It was Crazy Strips. Tons of Crazy Strips. Gazillions of Crazy Strips. A lifetime supply! At least ten boxes!

"Rare!" whispered Judy.

"Wow-wee!" said Rocky. "I've never seen so many Crazy Strips."

"I have," said Stink, pointing to Judy, Queen of the Crazy Strips. "But these are M-I-N-E, mine."

"You drew this?" asked Rocky, looking at Stink's design. "Double cool."

"Wow, your very own original Crazy Strip," said Judy. She couldn't help feeling like a green bean. *Green* with envy.

"Hey! Here's my sunglasses," said Stink, digging down to the bottom of the box. They were shaped like a Band-Aid. He put them on and looked at the sun. "They really work!" said Stink.

"Luck-y!" said Judy. "Those will protect you from that giant hole in the ozone over Antarctica."

Stink had his own Crazy Strip! Her very own batty little brother was now as famous as Josephine Dickson, Inventor of the Adhesive Bandage. If it weren't for that giant hole in the sky, she, Judy Moody, would move to Antarctica.

"Do you think they have bats in Antarctica?" Judy asked.

"Frozen bats," said Stink.

Ow-oooo! Judy tipped her head toward the ozone and let out one long howler-monkey howl.

Project P.E.N.C.I.L.

The next morning, and the next one after that, Judy woke up feeling like a sloth moth. She could hardly make herself get out of bed.

Saving the world was not going so well. She hadn't done anything *really* important. Like heal the world with her own Crazy Strip. So far, she had only saved four banana peels, a lunch bag, and a toad.

On Friday morning, Judy ate her no-garbage breakfast in silence. She packed her no-garbage lunch by herself. She didn't say a word when Stink stuck Crazy Strips all over his arms, elbows, knees, and chin.

"These Crazy Strips itch," said Stink, peeling off the one on his elbow. Judy couldn't stand it one more minute.

"If those were my Crazy Strips," said Judy, "I'd be happy to itch. I would not scratch once. And I would never not ever peel it off. Not even in the bathtub."

⚘   ⚘   ⚘

In school, Judy did not raise her hand once. She did not pass a note to Frank. She did nothing but chew her Grouchy pencil all through Spelling.

She, Judy Moody, was in a pencil-snapping mood.

When it was time for Science, Mr. Todd took off his watch and said, "I want everybody to sit still for sixty seconds. I'll time you." When the minute was up, Mr. Todd said, "In that minute, one hundred acres of trees in the rain forest were just destroyed.

That's seventy football fields."

"No way!" went through the class.

"We all depend on the rain forest," said Mr. Todd. "For things we eat and wear and use every single day. Think about it. Even your wooden pencil and rubber eraser could be from the rain forest. Ninety-eight percent of the cedar wood used for pencils comes from rain forest trees."

Judy stopped chewing on her Grouchy pencil. She stared at it. The grouchy face looked even grouchier. This pencil used to be a tree. A rain forest tree!

She, Judy Moody, would never, ever use a pencil again.

Not even a Grouchy pencil.

"If we help save the rain forest, we help save the planet," said Mr. Todd.

Suddenly, Judy had a plan. A perfect Save-the-World plan. All she had to do was skip recess.

When all the kids hurried outside to the playground, Judy sneaked back to the classroom. This was her big chance. Inside each desk was a pencil holder. Judy raced around the room and took the pencils from each desk. Then she hid them inside the flower vase.

As soon as recess was over, it was time for Math. "Take out your workbooks," said Mr. Todd. "Let's get those pencils working."

Uh-oh! Judy thought.

"Hey, my pencil's gone!"

"Mine too!"

"Mine was right here!"

"Mr. Todd! Mr. Todd! Somebody stole our pencils!" The whole class was in an uproar.

"Okay, is somebody playing a joke?" asked Mr. Todd. Nobody answered. "Do any of you know anything about the missing pencils?"

Judy kept her head down and pretended to work out math problems. Brad looked at Judy. She was the only one NOT complaining about her missing pencil. And she was doing math problems with a *p-e-n.*

"Pencil thief!" Brad yelled, pointing at her. "Judy Moody stole our pencils!"

Judy felt the eyes of twenty-one third-grade pencil lovers turn to glare at her.

"Judy?" Mr. Todd came over to her desk. "What do you know about these missing pencils?"

"Okay, I took them," Judy confessed. "Because I think we should stop using pencils."

"Stop using pencils? That's nuts!" Brad said.

"To help save the rain forest," said Judy.

"Hmm. Class, what do you think?" asked Mr. Todd.

"We just want our pencils back," said Leo.

Judy could not believe these third-grade pencil freaks! Were they in the ozone? Didn't they care that seventy football fields of trees a minute were being cut down? She wished they would all move to PENCILvania.

"I think we *should* save the rain forest," said Frank.

"Me too," said Hailey.

"Me three," Rocky said.

"Yeah, but we can't just give up pencils forever," said Randi. "We have to write stuff, and erase. Like in Math. How can we save the world without math?"

"Maybe we don't have to use so many," said Jessica Finch. "One pencil can draw a line thirty-five miles long. We could all promise to use the same pencil until fifth grade."

How did Jessica Fink Finch know so much

about pencils? Maybe she wasn't such a fink after all.

"How many pencils can you get from a tree?" Judy asked.

"None," said Brad. "Pencils don't grow on trees."

"Hardee-har-har," said Judy. "I mean it. You can get a lot of pencils from one tree. For real."

"One tree can make 172,000 pencils!" said Jessica Finch. "I read it in my *Ranger Rick* magazine."

"Wow! One tree could make all the pencils in our school."

"All the pencils in Virginia!"

"We could plant a tree in the rain forest, then," said Judy. "You know, for the Virginia Dare School. To make up for all the pencils we use."

"Kids all over the world raise money to protect rain forests," Jessica told the class. "It only costs a dollar to have one tree planted in the Children's Rain Forest in Costa Rica."

"If it only costs a dollar," Judy said, "then we could send money for them to plant trees, and our class can adopt them."

"Wow!" everybody said. "Let's do it."

"Class? Any ideas about how to raise some money?" Mr. Todd asked.

"How about a car wash?" said Lucy.

"We could sell stuff," said Adam. "Like cookies!"

"My sister put on a play in fifth grade and made money to help save the whales," said Jessica. "She even won a Giraffe Award for it."

A Giraffe Award! For somebody who sticks their neck out for a good cause. Judy could hardly wait till fifth grade!

"Maybe we could put on a magic show," said Rocky.

"Or we could collect a bunch of stuff to recycle," said Frank, "and get money for it. The Recycle Center gives five cents each for pop bottles and milk jugs."

"Rare!" said Judy.

"Double cool!" said Rocky.

"A bottle drive sounds like a fine idea," said Mr. Todd. "We could raise money while recycling at the same time. What do you say, class? Do you think we could collect enough bottles?"

"Yeah!" everybody yelled.

It was settled. The Virginia Dare School, Class 3T, was going into the bottle business. Starting with their very own cafeteria.

ⓔ   ⓔ   ⓔ

The third-graders spent the afternoon rounding up milk jugs from all over the school. They piled up plastic bottles from the kindergarten classes, and from the teachers' lunchroom. They even rescued some from the trash.

Class 3T worked as hard as an army of leaf-cutter ants. "That was cool how you got us out of Math," whispered Frank.

"This is more fun than when you put my arm in a cast," said Jessica.

"We still need a ton more bottles if we're going to save the rain forest," said Rocky.

"Rocky's right," said Mr. Todd. "Let's go home and see how many bottles we can collect over the weekend. Ask your family and neighbors. Tell your friends."

Judy Moody felt as sharp as a pencil point. They were just a few days and a few hundred bottles away from saving the rain forest.

She was in a Judy-Moody-best-mood-ever. At last she was on her way to saving the world. And the best part was she no longer had to do it all by herself. Class 3T would save the world together. Like an ecosystem!

She, Judy Monarch Moody, knew just how a butterfly felt coming out of the chrysalis. Light as a feather.

Batty for Bottles

"Let's go on a bottle hunt," said Rocky. "After school."

"I sure hope bottles are easier to find than northeast beach tiger beetles," Judy said.

They raided Rocky's garage first and found two milk crates full of bottles that had not been recycled. "Rare!" said Judy. "Twenty-seven bottles!"

"But they're all smooshed. I forgot my mom stomps them."

"That's okay," said Judy. "They're ABC bottles. Already Been Crushed!"

At Judy's, her mother let her have the stash of milk jugs she was saving to make bird feeders. Dad didn't have any bottles, so he gave Rocky and Judy one dollar bill each to plant a tree.

"Thanks, Mr. Moody!" said Rocky.

Judy kissed George Washington right on his presidential nose.

"Does this mean I can wear lipstick again?" asked Mom.

"And I can drink coffee?" said Dad.

"Yes. But not too much," laughed Judy.

"No fair," said Stink. "I'd plant a tree, too, if I could have a dollar or something."

"Or something," said Judy.

All the next week, Class 3T piled up a mountain of bottles in the multipurpose room. Bags of bottles, boxes of bottles, bins full of bottles. "Great teamwork, class," said Mr. Todd. "Did you know we throw away two and a half million plastic bottles every hour in this country? In three months, we throw away enough bottles to circle the globe."

"Look out!" said Rocky. "Bottles are taking over the earth!"

"People should recycle them," said

Jessica Finch. "My dad has a jacket made out of recycled plastic bottles. My socks are made out of bottles, too."

"No way," said Judy. She turned around to take a look at the plastic-bottle socks. They looked regular. They did not look plastic at all.

"It's true," said Mr. Todd. "All that plastic can be recycled to make toys and coat hangers and picture frames. Even recycling bins!"

"How many bottles do you think we have so far?" asked Jessica.

"Let's pile them up all together to see how high they go," said Brad.

Class 3T spent their Math class piling up bottles and more bottles.

"We should call it Bottle Mountain," said Rocky.

"Double cool," said Frank. "It looks like a giant igloo."

When they had added every last bottle, Mr. Todd said, "Tomorrow's the big day. Tomorrow we'll find out the grand total number of bottles we have. Our principal, Ms. Tuxedo, will make an announcement to tell the school how much money we've raised. Now let's hurry back to class so nobody misses the bus."

"Tomorrow!" said Judy. "That's twenty-four more hours!" She couldn't wait to find out how many trees would be planted in the rain forest for the Virginia Dare School.

The Winking Disease

When Judy and Rocky stepped off the bus on Friday morning, Ms. Tuxedo was standing outside the school doors. "How's it going, you two?"

"Pretty good, I guess," said Judy.

"Today we find out how many trees we're going to plant," said Rocky.

"That's right," the principal said. "You both have a good day." And she winked. Judy looked at Rocky. Rocky looked at Judy.

In Judy Moody's entire third-grade life, she was sure she had never seen the principal wink at anybody.

Judy and Rocky hurried to the multi-purpose room before class to look at the mountain of bottles again, but the doors were locked. When they got to 3T, Mr. Todd was standing in the doorway. "Isn't it a lovely Friday?" he said. Then he winked. In Judy Moody's entire third-grade life, she had never heard Mr. Todd say the word *lovely*. And for sure and absolute positive, she had never seen him wink.

"Something's up," she told Rocky.

Judy sat down next to Frank. "Know what? Something's funny. All the teachers have a winking disease today."

"A winking disease?"

"Yeah, you know, when they wink at you and say nice things."

While Judy waited for the day to begin, she looked around the room at all the kids in her ecosystem. Not one third-grader was absent. And every single person in Class 3T had pitched in and collected bottles.

"Class," said Mr. Todd, blinking the lights to get their attention. "Announcements. Listen up."

Judy Moody squirmed all through morning announcements. A Mexican jumping bean could have done a better job of sitting still.

"And now," came Ms. Tuxedo's voice over the PA system, "the moment you've been waiting for . . ." Judy Moody sat up super straight and used her best third-grade listening ears.

"As you know, Mr. Todd's room, Class 3T, has been collecting bottles this week to raise money for the rain forest. This money will go, on behalf of the Virginia Dare School, to plant trees in the Children's Rain Forest in Costa Rica. Thanks to Class 3T, the Virginia Dare School has collected 1,961 bottles. That means we will be planting ninety-eight trees to help save the rain forest."

Ninety-eight! Suddenly, Judy remembered the dollars from her dad. Two more dollars meant two more trees. One hundred trees! Class 3T went wild, jumping up and down, clapping and whooping and hooting like owls.

"We'd like to show our appreciation to our third graders in a special assembly today at 2:30. This will provide the whole school with a chance to give them a big hand and show them how proud we are of their hard work and their efforts for such a good cause."

"Lunch today is Sloppy Joes," Ms. Tuxedo continued. "Tickets go on sale Monday for the school fair. And will Judy Moody please report to the front office?"

"Uh-oh. Judy's in trouble," Jessica Finch said.

"Nobody's in trouble," said Mr. Todd. "Judy's going to represent our class at the assembly today. After all, she got us thinking about our pencils, and before we knew it, we were planting trees in the rain forest. Judy, go ahead down to the office and find out what Ms. Tuxedo would like you to do."

Judy walked as fast as she could without running down the great green halls of the Virginia Dare School to the front office. The third-grade papier-mâché masks outside the classroom seemed to wink at her. The second-grade self-portraits grinned. And the first-grade sunflowers on the wall stood up prouder.

Ms. Tuxedo took Judy into the multi-purpose room. The principal showed Judy where to sit in the front row and told her when to come up on stage.

"When I call you up on stage, I'll hand you something for your class. You accept it, then walk across the stage and rejoin your class."

"Is it a certificate?" asked Judy.

"It's a surprise! It'll be fun. You'll see," said the principal. And she winked. So *this* is what all the winking is about, Judy thought.

At 2:25, Mr. Todd's class hurried to the multipurpose room. Judy took her seat in the front row.

The room was dark. The curtains went up. A single spotlight shone on Ms. Tuxedo. Everybody clapped.

"Today, boys and girls, we are here to show how proud we are of Class 3T. They showed excellent teamwork on a project raising money to plant trees in the Children's Rain Forest in Costa Rica. Because of them, one hundred trees will be planted for the Virginia Dare School. Margaret Mead says, 'Never doubt that a small group of concerned people can change the world.' Our special thanks to 3T for helping to change the world!"

Everybody cheered and clapped some more.

"Ranger Piner is here as our special guest from the County Parks Department. They have donated a cedar tree, like the ones in the rain forest, to the Virginia Dare School.

Right after the assembly, Ranger Piner will help Mr. Todd's class plant the tree in front of our school.

"To show our appreciation, I have here, for every member of the class, a T-shirt and a gift certificate for one free Rain Forest Mist ice-cream cone from Screamin' Mimi's." Ms. Tuxedo waved an envelope in the air, and held up one of the T-shirts. It said TURN PLASTIC INTO TREES under a picture of a tree made out of bottles.

Judy's class jumped up and down and hooted some more. A T-shirt with words! And the kind of certificate that got you a free ice cream! Saving the world was even better than Judy thought.

"There's one person who proved to be a good friend to the whole planet and I'd like her to come up on stage — Judy Moody!"

Judy looked back at Mr. Todd. He motioned for her to go up on stage.

Judy Moody stood in the bright beam of light and tried not to squint. She looked out at all her classmates from 3T who had helped plant trees to save the rain forest. They waved their hands in the air and gave a howler-monkey hoot.

Ms. Tuxedo continued. "Usually this award goes to one fifth-grade student, but today, I think the whole third-grade class is deserving."

Award! Judy stood up straighter.

"Class 3T has made a contribution that will help not only our community, but the larger community — our planet, our world. Judy Moody and Class 3T, let me present — the award for somebody who really sticks their neck out — the Giraffe Award!"

The Giraffe! Judy could not believe her ears. Even her best third-grade listening ears. Everybody wanted to be a Giraffe when they got to fifth grade. She, Judy Moody, was a Giraffe in third grade!

Ms. Tuxedo handed her a gold trophy of a giraffe. "Let's give a big hand for 3T!"

Then, all of the third-grade Giraffes came up on stage to join hands and get their pictures taken in their new bottle-tree T-shirts. Cameras snapped and bulbs flashed. One of the cameras was Dad!

Dad reached up to give Judy a hug. "I brought the car," said Dad. "Thought I'd help take bottles to the Recycling Center after school."

"Rare!" said Judy.

"We're proud of you, kiddo," said Dad. "All of you."

Judy smiled. Not a Siberian-tiger smile. A real smile. The kind the dentist would really miss seeing.

Class 3T had joined together to make a difference. One hundred brand-new trees would be planted, like a Band-Aid for the rain forest. And she, Judy Moody, had played a small part in saving the world.

Judy stood in the center of the 3T ecosystem. She held the trophy high, and stretched her neck tall as a true Giraffe.

Megan McDonald is the author of the award-winning *Judy Moody* and *Judy Moody Gets Famous!* and numerous other books for children. After writing *Judy Moody Gets Famous!*, she confessed, "Okay. I admit it. I am Judy Moody. Same-same! In my family of sisters, we're famous for exaggeration. Judy Moody is me . . . exaggerated!" Megan McDonald lives with her husband in northern California, with two dogs, two adopted horses, and fifteen wild turkeys.

Peter Reynolds is the illustrator of all three Judy Moody books. Of *Judy Moody Saves the World!* he says, "It was almost spooky that I painted the cover on the morning of September 11, 2001. I looked at what I was painting, and the words jumped out at me in a new and more meaningful way. JUDY MOODY SAVES THE WORLD! Judy shows that she can channel her feisty energy to make the world a better place. I hope this special book will inspire the next generation to 'save the world' too." Peter Reynolds lives in Dedham, Massachusetts.